NIGEL'S NIGHT OUT

First published in Australia by Collins/Angus
& Robertson Publishers Australia 1991
First published in Picture Lions 1992

Picture Lions is an imprint of the Children's Division,
part of HarperCollins Publishers Limited,
77-85 Fulham Palace Road, Hammersmith,
London W6 8JB

Printed in Great Britain by
BPCC Hazell Books, Paulton and Aylesbury

NIGEL'S NIGHT OUT

DONNI CARTER

PictureLions

An Imprint of HarperCollins*Publishers*

'I'm glad we're eating out tonight,'
said Mum to her new boyfriend.
'Nigel's been horrible all day.'

'Been a bit of a *monster*, has he?'

'I've been wanting to try this new Bistro,' said Mum.

BEASTro?

'I'm going to the toilet,'
said Nigel.

'Okay,' said Mum,
'but come right back.'

ZAP!

'I'm sorry I was such a monster today, Mum,' said Nigel.
'I'll be better tomorrow.'

'If you're good,' said Mum,
'maybe we'll go to the zoo.'